Cecil's Garden

by
Holly Keller

Greenwillow Books · An Imprint of HarperCollinsPublishers

Cecil's Garden
Copyright © 2002 by Holly Keller
All rights reserved. Printed in Hong Kong
by South China Printing Company (1988) Ltd.
www.harperchildrens.com

Black line and watercolor paints were used for the full-color art.
The text type is Futura Book.

Library of Congress Cataloging-in-Publication Data
Keller, Holly.
Cecil's garden / by Holly Keller.
p.   cm.
"Greenwillow Books."
Summary: After seeing how arguing affects the other
animals, Cecil figures out how to plant a garden that he
and his friends can all enjoy.
ISBN 0-06-029593-7 (trade). ISBN 0-06-029594-5 (lib. bdg.)
[1. Behavior—Fiction. 2. Rabbits—Fiction. 3. Animals—Fiction.
4. Gardening—Fiction.]   I. Title.
PZ7.K28132 Ce 2002 [E]—dc21 2001016029

10 9 8 7 6 5 4 3 2 1
First Edition

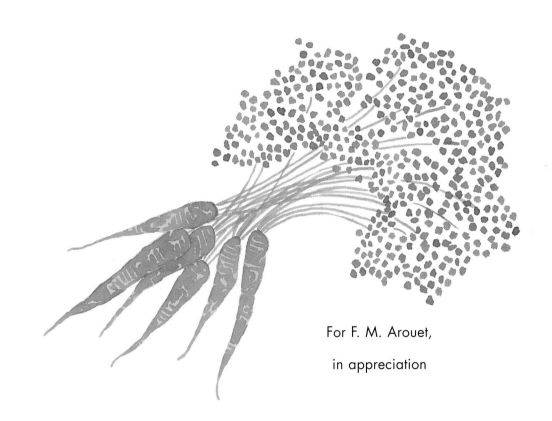

For F. M. Arouet,

in appreciation

Cecil opened his eyes and jumped out of bed.
It was the day he was going to help Jake and Posey
plant the vegetable garden.
He stuck his nose outside and took a deep breath.
"Perfect," he said.

Jake carried the hoe and the shovel.
Posey brought the watering can.
"You get the seeds, Cecil," Posey said,
and he did.

Jake turned over the soil, and Posey dug the rows.

Cecil looked at the beautiful pictures on the seed packages.
"We have carrots and peas, beans, lettuce, brussels sprouts,
and squash," he said, and his mouth began to water.
"That's six kinds of seeds," said Jake, "and the garden is
only big enough for five rows."

"Nobody likes brussels sprouts," said Posey. "We don't have
to plant those."

"I like brussels sprouts," Jake said. "We can leave out the
squash."

"But I love squash," said Cecil.

"I know," said Posey. "Let's plant two vegetables in one row."

"How about carrots with peas?" said Cecil. "That sounds good."

Posey shook her head. "I think it should be beans and lettuce."

They argued until the sun was high in the sky and it was too hot to work. Posey picked up the watering can, Jake took the hoe and the shovel, and they all went back to the house. Cecil was still holding the seeds, because they hadn't planted anything.

He was very disappointed.

When he was feeling better, Cecil decided to take a walk.
A bird was singing, and Cecil started to sing too.
"I think I'll go to visit Mouse," he said to himself, and he
started down the path.

He went around a curve, squeezed through some
tangled bushes, and was very surprised
to find himself standing in front of a saucepan.
Mouse and some of his friends were in it.
The pan was full of bath toys, and the mice were
making a terrible racket.
Cecil covered his ears.
"Hello, Mouse," he shouted. "What are you doing?"
"We're taking a bath," Mouse yelled. "What does it
 look like?"
"But you don't have any water," Cecil shouted back.
"No," yelled Mouse. "We dumped it out."

Cecil giggled, and Mouse climbed out of the pan. "You might think it's funny, Cecil," Mouse said, "but it isn't. We try to take a bath every Saturday, and every Saturday it's always the same. We fill the pan with water, and then we get our toys. But after we put the toys in, there's never any room left for us. And since we can never agree on which toys to take out, we always have to take out the water."

"And then we all fit," said one of the other mice.

"But we don't get very clean."

"Oh, dear," said Cecil, trying not to laugh. "Maybe next Saturday will be better."

"I doubt it," said Mouse, and Cecil helped him get back into the pan.

"Perhaps this isn't the best time for a visit," said Cecil.

"I'll come back on a different day, and I'll go to the moles' house now."

When Cecil got to the moles' house,
he knocked on the door.
There wasn't any answer, so he opened
the door a crack and peeked in.
It was dark inside, and the mole family were still in their pajamas.
Angus was standing in front of a clock, and he was peering at
it intently.

"Hello, Angus," Cecil said in a loudish whisper. "Why are you still in your pajamas on such a nice morning?"
Angus jumped, because he hadn't seen Cecil.
"Is it morning?" Angus asked.
"Yes," said Cecil. "Well, no," he corrected himself. "It's really almost lunchtime."
"I was sure that it was time to get up," Angus said, "but it's too dark in here to see the clock."

Violet giggled.

"Even if you could see the clock, Angus," she said, "you don't know how to tell time."

"I don't need to tell time," Angus protested. "I always know in my bones when it's time to get up."

"Well, I always know in my bones when it's time to get back into bed," she said, and she pulled the blanket up to her nose.

"Maybe we should eat breakfast," said Margaret, because she was hungry.

"There's no point in eating breakfast if it's time for lunch," Angus said.

Cecil was getting a headache.

"All this quarreling seems to me to be a foolish waste of time, whatever time it is," he said.

"It *is* a waste of time," said Violet from under the covers, "but we're not in a hurry, so we have plenty."

"Well," said Cecil, "I'm running out of time. Today is the day Posey, Jake, and I are supposed to plant our vegetable garden, and I am going straight home to do it."

Cecil walked as fast as he could.
How beautiful our garden will be, he thought.

"Where have you been?" asked Jake when Cecil came
through the door.
"Visiting the neighbors," Cecil answered, and he went
to get the seeds and the toolbox.
"Where are you going now?" asked Posey.
"To the garden," said Cecil. "You bring the watering can,
and Jake, you bring the shovel and the hoe."

When they got to the garden, Cecil started to work
on the fence.
He moved two posts and added more wire so that
the garden would be bigger.

"There," he said when he was finished. "Now we have room for everything. There is nothing to quarrel about, and we don't have to waste another minute."

Posey and Jake agreed that it was a very good solution. They planted seeds until the sun was setting pink and orange over the meadow.

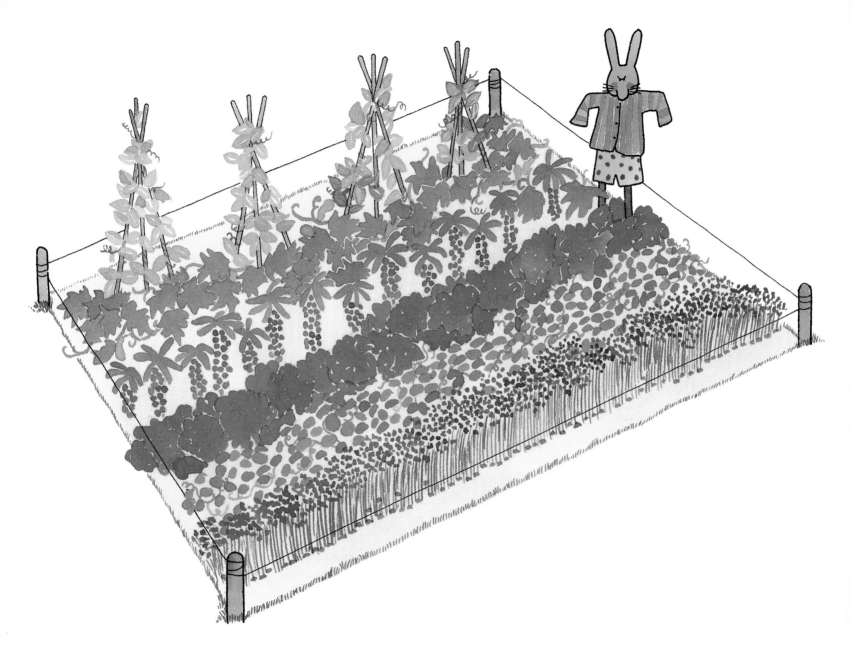

By the middle of summer the garden was full of beautiful vegetables.

Cecil made a pot of savory stew and invited
the mice and the moles to lunch.

Mouse wrote a note saying that they were really too dirty to come to a party, and the moles sent regrets because they just couldn't find the time.

So Posey, Jake, and Cecil ate the stew all by themselves.

And it was very good.